DATE DUE

D1272239

STAR WARS®

EPISODE VI
RETURN OF THE JEDI™

VOLUME FOUR

SCRIPT
ARCHIE GOODWIN

ART
AL WILLIAMSON
CARLOS GARZÓN

COLORS
CARY PORTER
PERRY McNAMEE

LETTERING
ED KING

COVER ART
RODOLFO MIGLIARI

DARK HORSE COMICS

Spotlight

VISIT US AT
www.abdopublishing.com

Reinforced library bound edition published in 2010 by Spotlight, a division of the ABDO Group, 8000 West 78th Street, Edina, Minnesota 55439. Spotlight produces high-quality reinforced library bound editions for schools and libraries. Published by agreement with Dark Horse Comics, Inc., and Lucasfilm Ltd.

Printed in the United States of America, Melrose Park, Illinois.
092009
012010

 PRINTED ON RECYCLED PAPER

Library of Congress Cataloging-in-Publication Data

Goodwin, Archie.
  Episode VI : return of the Jedi / based on the screenplay by George
Lucas ; script adaptation Archie Goodwin ; artists Al Williamson &
Carlos Garzon ; letterer Ed King. -- Reinforced library bound ed.
      p. cm. -- (Star wars)
  "Dark Horse Comics."
  ISBN 978-1-59961-705-3 (vol. 1) -- ISBN 978-1-59961-706-0 (vol. 2)
-- ISBN 978-1-59961-707-7 (vol. 3) -- ISBN 978-1-59961-708-4 (vol. 4)
  1. Graphic novels. [1. Graphic novels.] I. Lucas, George, 1944- II.
Williamson, Al, 1931- III. Garzon, Carlos. IV. Return of the Jedi
(Motion picture) V. Title. VI. Title: Episode six. VII. Title: Return of the
Jedi.
  PZ7.7.G656Epk 2010
  [Fic]--dc22
                              2009030862

All Spotlight books have reinforced library bindings and
are manufactured in the United States of America.

Episode VI

RETURN OF THE JEDI™

Volume 4

The Rebel Alliance has begun their greatest strike against the Empire, sending Princess Leia, Luke Skywalker, and Han Solo to Endor, where they hope to deactivate the energy shield protecting the second Death Star.

The team avoids Imperial detection, and with the help of C-3P0 becomes allies with the residents of Endor, the Ewoks.

Feeling he may expose the Rebels because Darth Vader can sense him through the Force, Luke makes a decision to leave and confront Vader, hoping to return the dark lord to the light side.

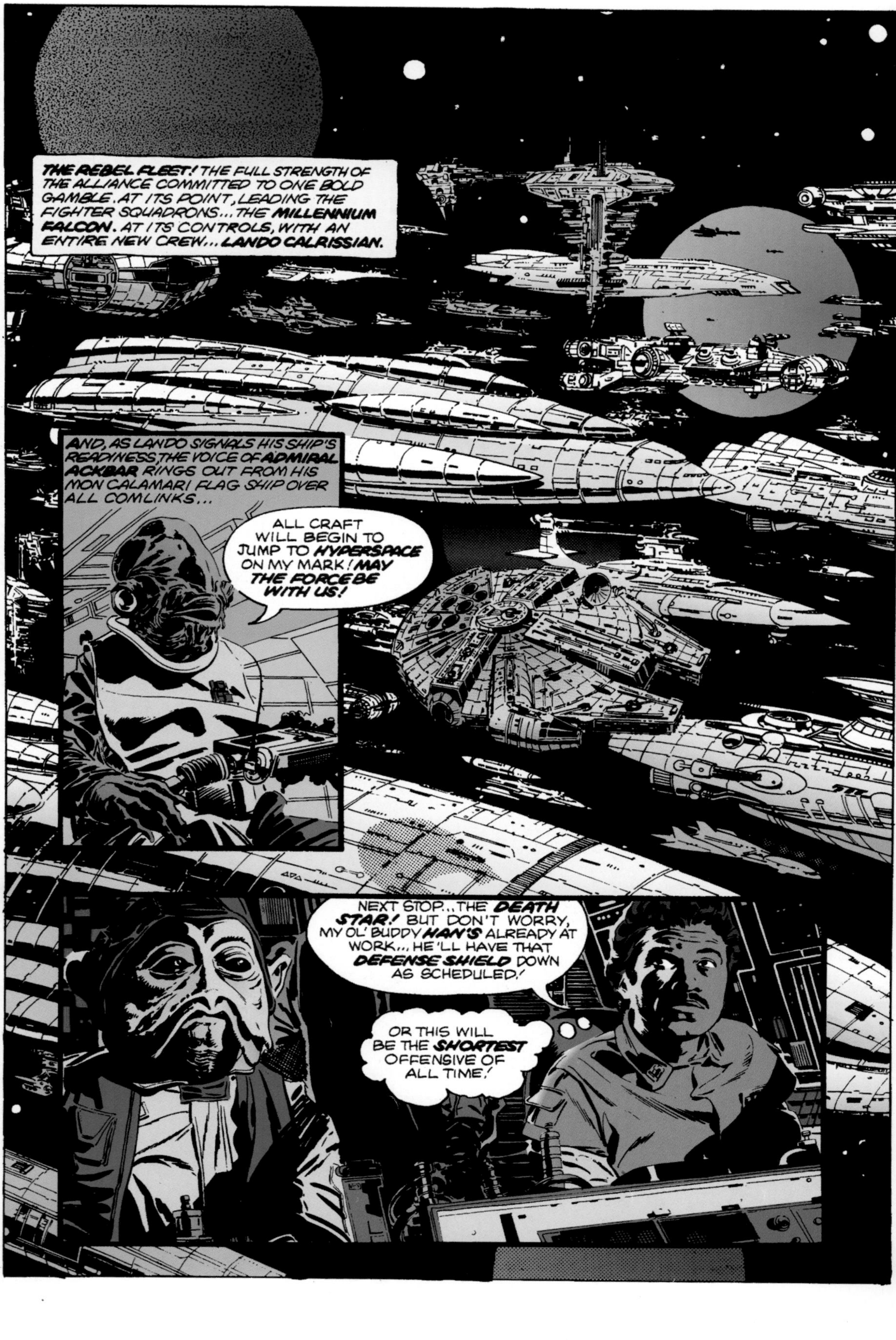
THE REBEL FLEET! THE FULL STRENGTH OF THE ALLIANCE COMMITTED TO ONE BOLD GAMBLE. AT ITS POINT, LEADING THE FIGHTER SQUADRONS... THE MILLENNIUM FALCON. AT ITS CONTROLS, WITH AN ENTIRE NEW CREW... LANDO CALRISSIAN.
AND, AS LANDO SIGNALS HIS SHIP'S READINESS, THE VOICE OF ADMIRAL ACKBAR RINGS OUT FROM HIS MON CALAMARI FLAG SHIP OVER ALL COMLINKS...
ALL CRAFT WILL BEGIN TO JUMP TO HYPERSPACE ON MY MARK! MAY THE FORCE BE WITH US!
NEXT STOP... THE DEATH STAR! BUT DON'T WORRY, MY OL' BUDDY HAN'S ALREADY AT WORK... HE'LL HAVE THAT DEFENSE SHIELD DOWN AS SCHEDULED!
OR THIS WILL BE THE SHORTEST OFFENSIVE OF ALL TIME!

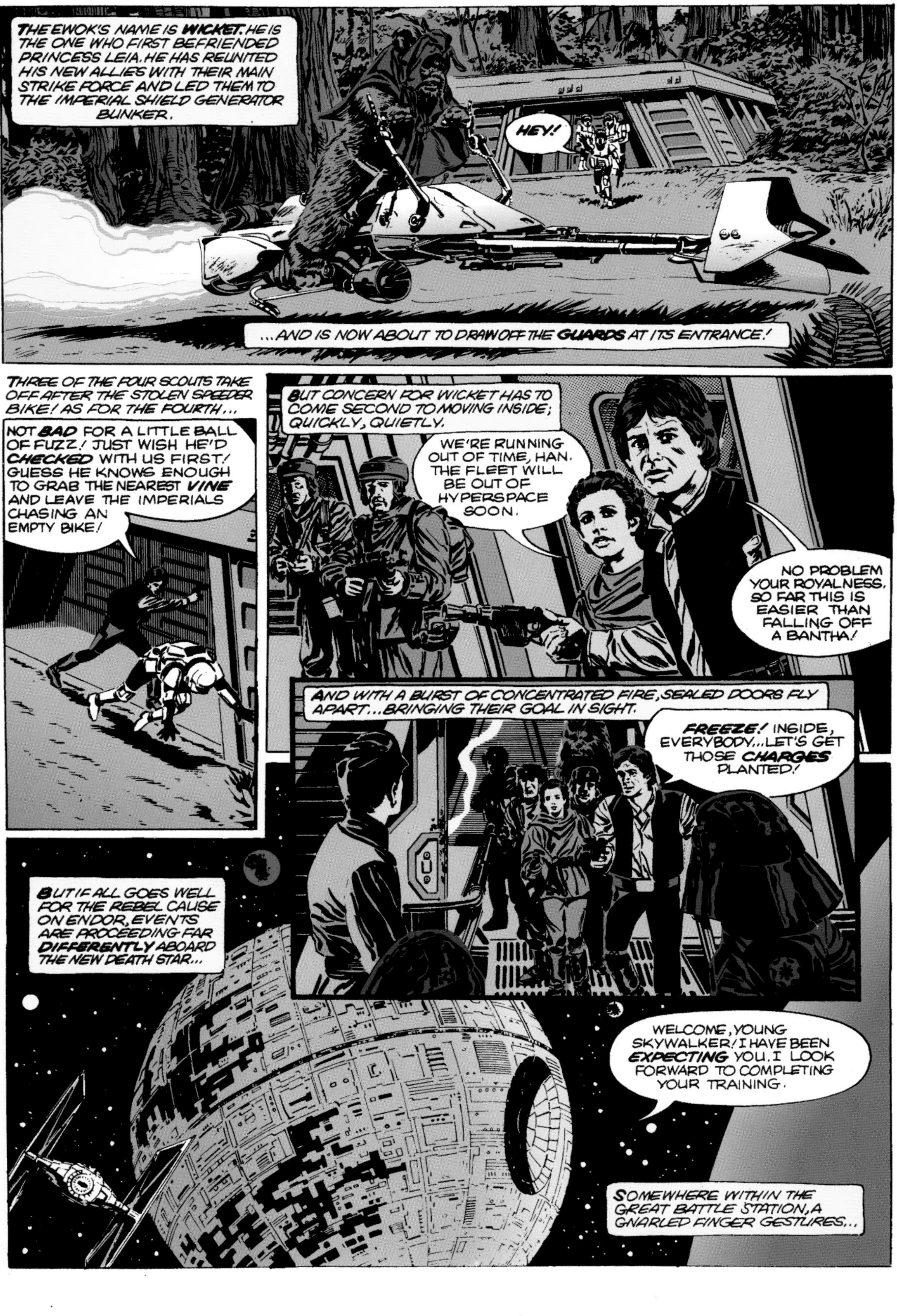
THE EWOK'S NAME IS WICKET. HE IS THE ONE WHO FIRST BEFRIENDED PRINCESS LEIA. HE HAS REUNITED HIS NEW ALLIES WITH THEIR MAIN STRIKE FORCE AND LED THEM TO THE IMPERIAL SHIELD GENERATOR BUNKER.
HEY!!
...AND IS NOW ABOUT TO DRAW OFF THE GUARDS AT ITS ENTRANCE!
THREE OF THE FOUR SCOUTS TAKE OFF AFTER THE STOLEN SPEEDER BIKE! AS FOR THE FOURTH...
NOT BAD FOR A LITTLE BALL OF FUZZ! JUST WISH HE'D CHECKED WITH US FIRST! GUESS HE KNOWS ENOUGH TO GRAB THE NEAREST VINE AND LEAVE THE IMPERIALS CHASING AN EMPTY BIKE!
BUT CONCERN FOR WICKET HAS TO COME SECOND TO MOVING INSIDE; QUICKLY, QUIETLY.
WE'RE RUNNING OUT OF TIME, HAN. THE FLEET WILL BE OUT OF HYPERSPACE SOON.
NO PROBLEM YOUR ROYALNESS. SO FAR THIS IS EASIER THAN FALLING OFF A BANTHA!
AND WITH A BURST OF CONCENTRATED FIRE, SEALED DOORS FLY APART... BRINGING THEIR GOAL IN SIGHT.
FREEZE! INSIDE, EVERYBODY... LET'S GET THOSE CHARGES PLANTED!
BUT IF ALL GOES WELL FOR THE REBEL CAUSE ON ENDOR, EVENTS ARE PROCEEDING FAR DIFFERENTLY ABOARD THE NEW DEATH STAR...
WELCOME, YOUNG SKYWALKER! I HAVE BEEN EXPECTING YOU. I LOOK FORWARD TO COMPLETING YOUR TRAINING.
SOMEWHERE WITHIN THE GREAT BATTLE STATION, A GNARLED FINGER GESTURES...

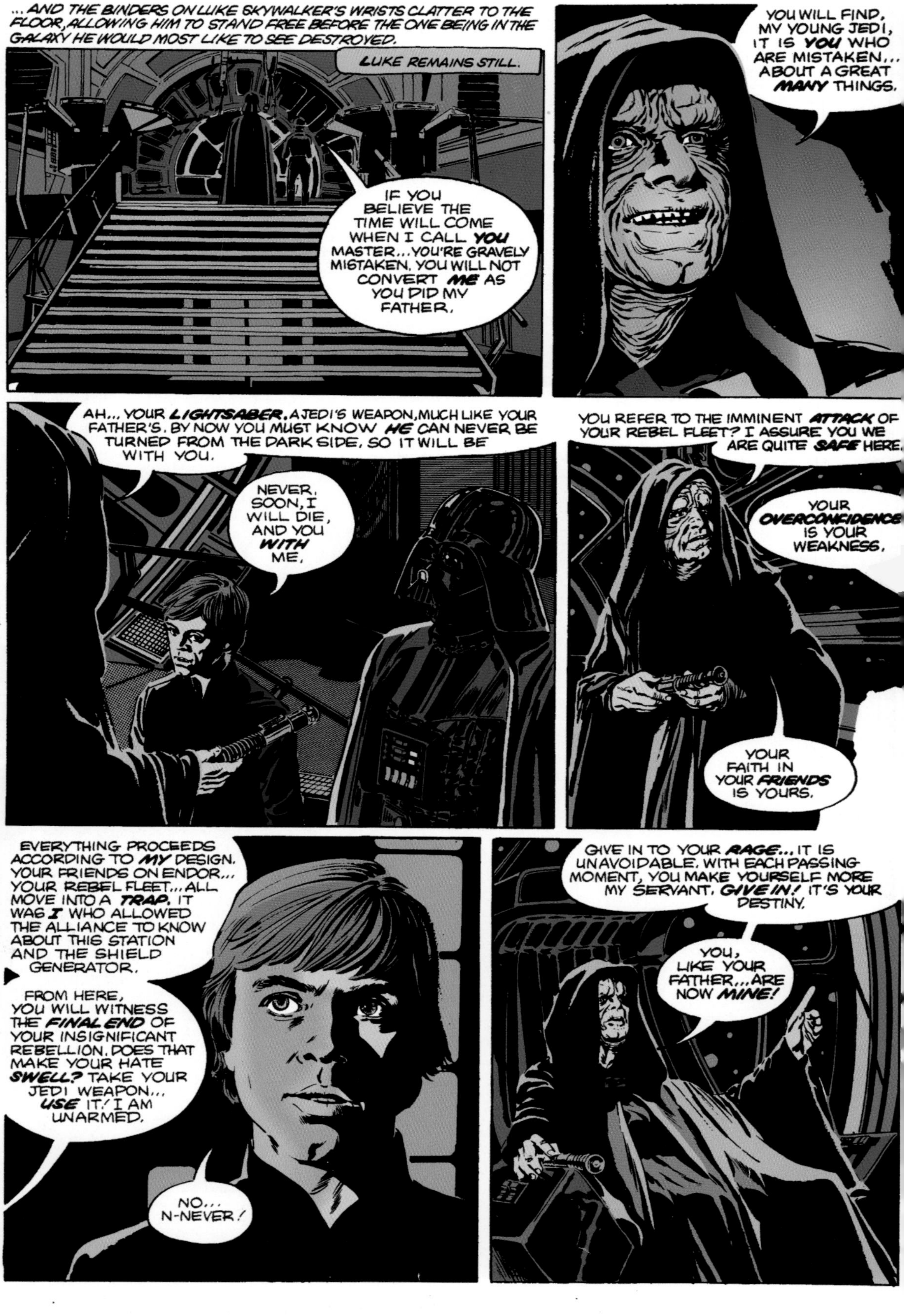

...AND THE BINDERS ON LUKE SKYWALKER'S WRISTS CLATTER TO THE FLOOR, ALLOWING HIM TO STAND FREE BEFORE THE ONE BEING IN THE GALAXY HE WOULD MOST LIKE TO SEE DESTROYED.
LUKE REMAINS STILL.
IF YOU BELIEVE THE TIME WILL COME WHEN I CALL YOU MASTER... YOU'RE GRAVELY MISTAKEN. YOU WILL NOT CONVERT ME AS YOU DID MY FATHER.
YOU WILL FIND, MY YOUNG JEDI, IT IS YOU WHO ARE MISTAKEN... ABOUT A GREAT MANY THINGS.
AH... YOUR LIGHTSABER. A JEDI'S WEAPON, MUCH LIKE YOUR FATHER'S. BY NOW YOU MUST KNOW HE CAN NEVER BE TURNED FROM THE DARK SIDE, SO IT WILL BE WITH YOU.
NEVER. SOON, I WILL DIE, AND YOU WITH ME.
YOU REFER TO THE IMMINENT ATTACK OF YOUR REBEL FLEET? I ASSURE YOU WE ARE QUITE SAFE HERE.
YOUR OVERCONFIDENCE IS YOUR WEAKNESS.
YOUR FAITH IN YOUR FRIENDS IS YOURS.
EVERYTHING PROCEEDS ACCORDING TO MY DESIGN. YOUR FRIENDS ON ENDOR... YOUR REBEL FLEET... ALL MOVE INTO A TRAP. IT WAS I WHO ALLOWED THE ALLIANCE TO KNOW ABOUT THIS STATION AND THE SHIELD GENERATOR.
FROM HERE, YOU WILL WITNESS THE FINAL END OF YOUR INSIGNIFICANT REBELLION. DOES THAT MAKE YOUR HATE SWELL? TAKE YOUR JEDI WEAPON... USE IT! I AM UNARMED.
NO... N-NEVER!
GIVE IN TO YOUR RAGE... IT IS UNAVOIDABLE. WITH EACH PASSING MOMENT, YOU MAKE YOURSELF MORE MY SERVANT. GIVE IN! IT'S YOUR DESTINY.
YOU, LIKE YOUR FATHER... ARE NOW MINE!

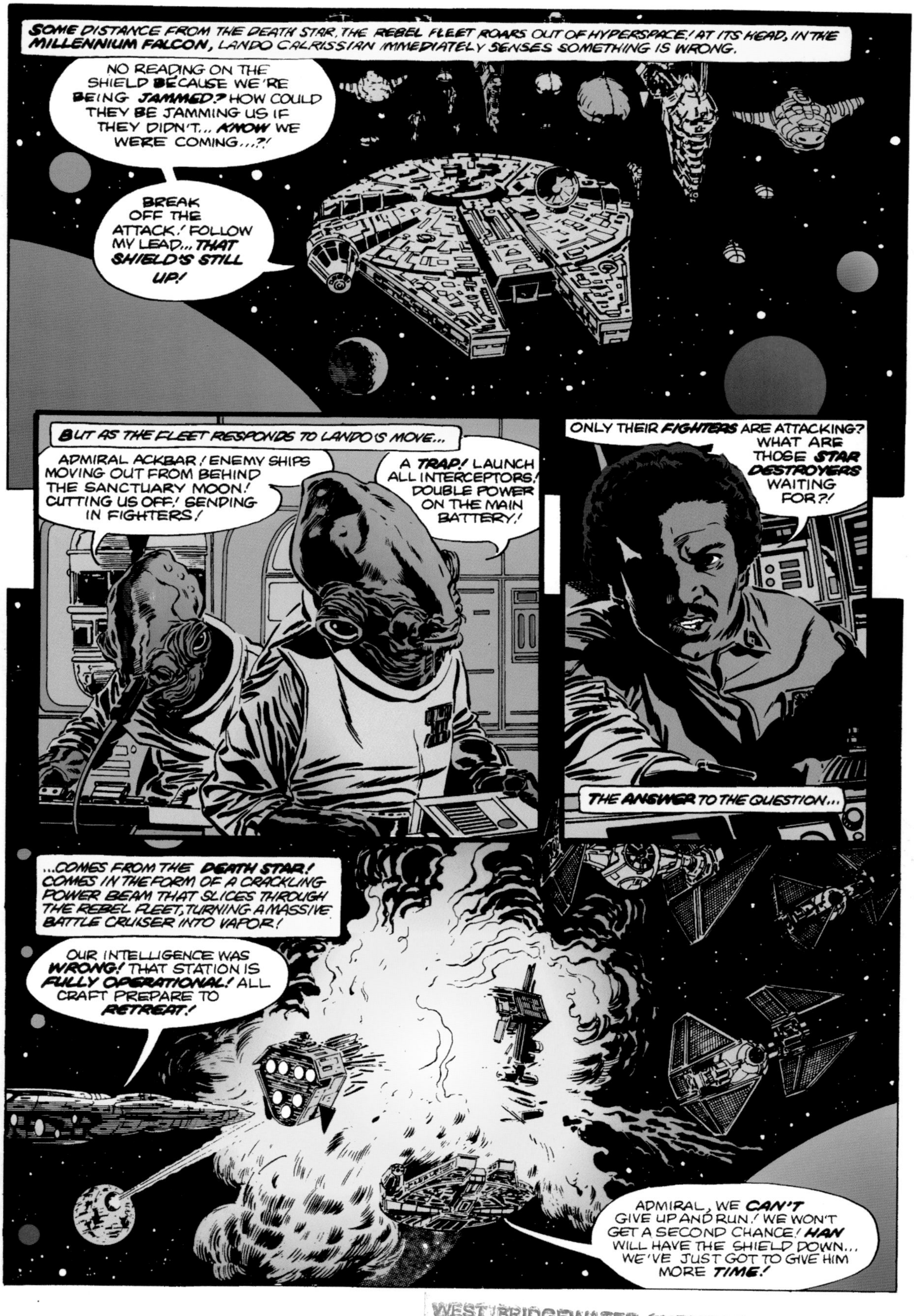
SOME DISTANCE FROM THE DEATH STAR, THE REBEL FLEET ROARS OUT OF HYPERSPACE! AT ITS HEAD, IN THE MILLENNIUM FALCON, LANDO CALRISSIAN IMMEDIATELY SENSES SOMETHING IS WRONG.
NO READING ON THE SHIELD BECAUSE WE'RE BEING JAMMED? HOW COULD THEY BE JAMMING US IF THEY DIDN'T... KNOW WE WERE COMING...?!
BREAK OFF THE ATTACK! FOLLOW MY LEAD... THAT SHIELD'S STILL UP!
BUT AS THE FLEET RESPONDS TO LANDO'S MOVE...
ADMIRAL ACKBAR! ENEMY SHIPS MOVING OUT FROM BEHIND THE SANCTUARY MOON! CUTTING US OFF! SENDING IN FIGHTERS!
A TRAP! LAUNCH ALL INTERCEPTORS! DOUBLE POWER ON THE MAIN BATTERY!
ONLY THEIR FIGHTERS ARE ATTACKING? WHAT ARE THOSE STAR DESTROYERS WAITING FOR?!
THE ANSWER TO THE QUESTION...
...COMES FROM THE DEATH STAR! COMES IN THE FORM OF A CRACKLING POWER BEAM THAT SLICES THROUGH THE REBEL FLEET, TURNING A MASSIVE BATTLE CRUISER INTO VAPOR!
OUR INTELLIGENCE WAS WRONG! THAT STATION IS FULLY OPERATIONAL! ALL CRAFT PREPARE TO RETREAT!
ADMIRAL, WE CAN'T GIVE UP AND RUN! WE WON'T GET A SECOND CHANCE! HAN WILL HAVE THE SHIELD DOWN... WE'VE JUST GOT TO GIVE HIM MORE TIME!

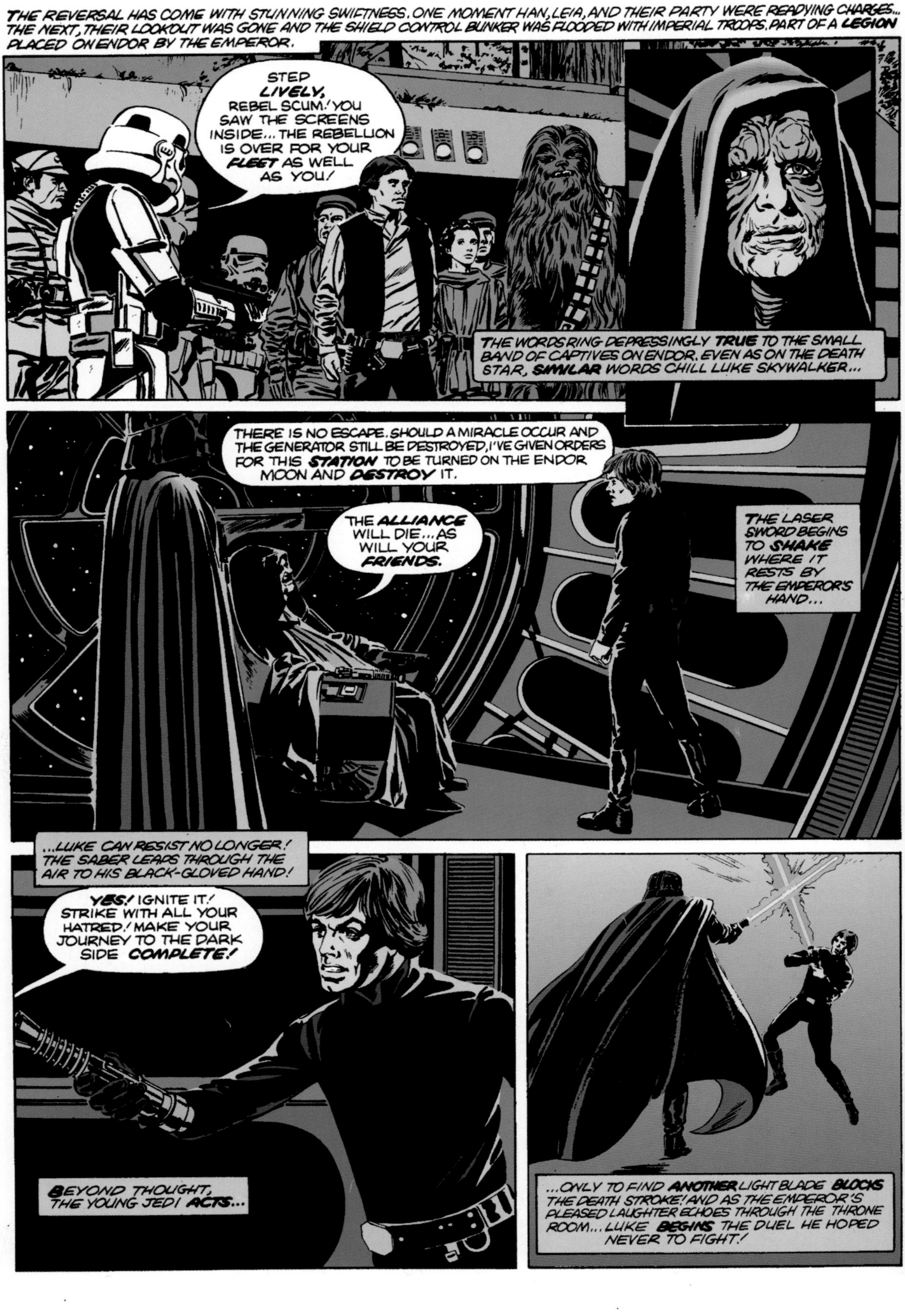
THE REVERSAL HAS COME WITH STUNNING SWIFTNESS. ONE MOMENT HAN, LEIA, AND THEIR PARTY WERE READYING CHARGES... THE NEXT, THEIR LOOKOUT WAS GONE AND THE SHIELD CONTROL BUNKER WAS FLOODED WITH IMPERIAL TROOPS, PART OF A LEGION PLACED ON ENDOR BY THE EMPEROR.
STEP LIVELY, REBEL SCUM! YOU SAW THE SCREENS INSIDE... THE REBELLION IS OVER FOR YOUR FLEET AS WELL AS YOU!
THE WORDS RING DEPRESSINGLY TRUE TO THE SMALL BAND OF CAPTIVES ON ENDOR. EVEN AS ON THE DEATH STAR, SIMILAR WORDS CHILL LUKE SKYWALKER...
THERE IS NO ESCAPE. SHOULD A MIRACLE OCCUR AND THE GENERATOR STILL BE DESTROYED, I'VE GIVEN ORDERS FOR THIS STATION TO BE TURNED ON THE ENDOR MOON AND DESTROY IT.
THE ALLIANCE WILL DIE... AS WILL YOUR FRIENDS.
THE LASER SWORD BEGINS TO SHAKE WHERE IT RESTS BY THE EMPEROR'S HAND...
...LUKE CAN RESIST NO LONGER! THE SABER LEAPS THROUGH THE AIR TO HIS BLACK-GLOVED HAND!
YES! IGNITE IT! STRIKE WITH ALL YOUR HATRED! MAKE YOUR JOURNEY TO THE DARK SIDE COMPLETE!
BEYOND THOUGHT, THE YOUNG JEDI ACTS...
...ONLY TO FIND ANOTHER LIGHT BLADE BLOCKS THE DEATH STROKE! AND AS THE EMPEROR'S PLEASED LAUGHTER ECHOES THROUGH THE THRONE ROOM... LUKE BEGINS THE DUEL HE HOPED NEVER TO FIGHT!

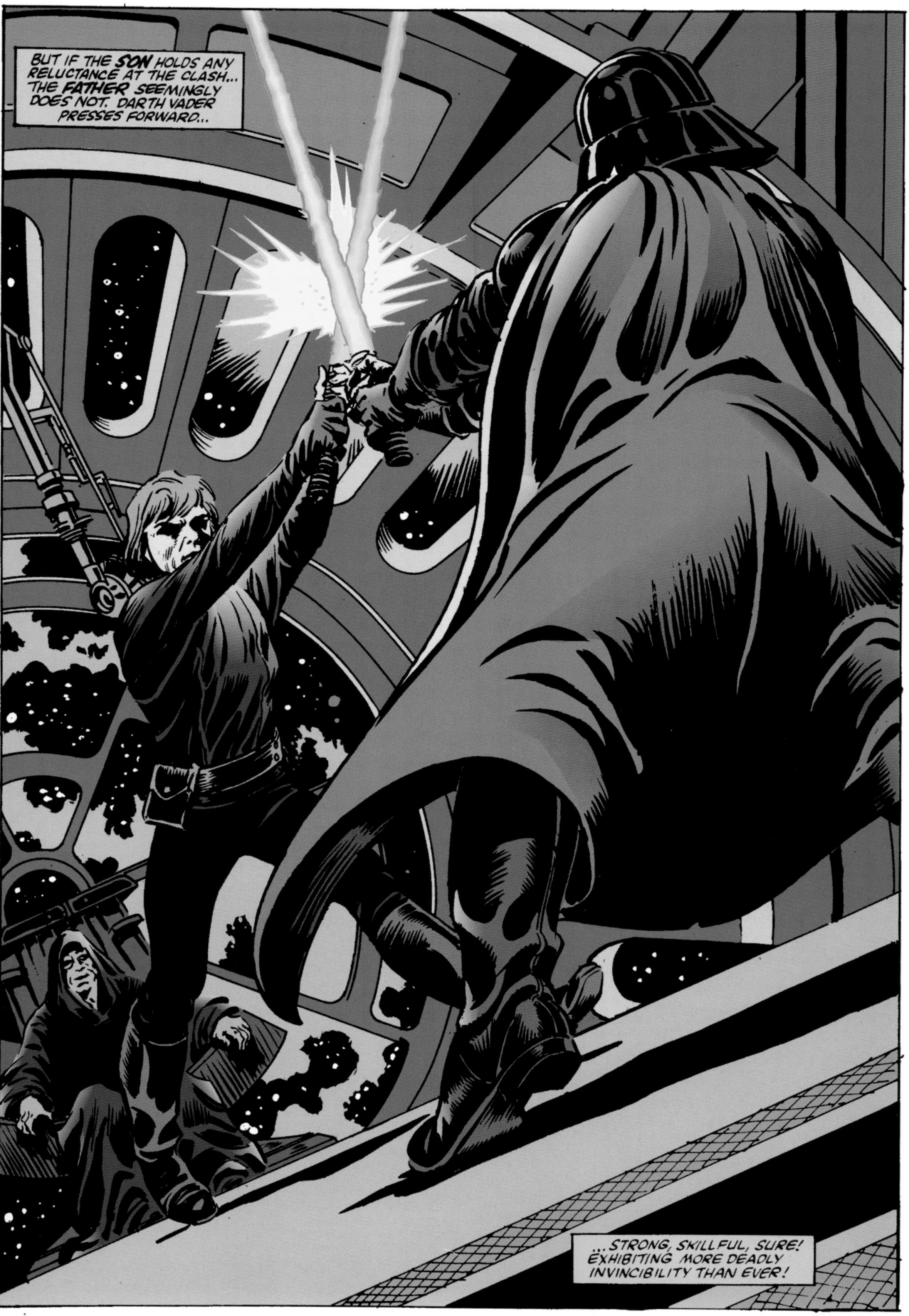
BUT IF THE SON HOLDS ANY RELUCTANCE AT THE CLASH... THE FATHER SEEMINGLY DOES NOT. DARTH VADER PRESSES FORWARD...
...STRONG, SKILLFUL, SURE! EXHIBITING MORE DEADLY INVINCIBILITY THAN EVER!

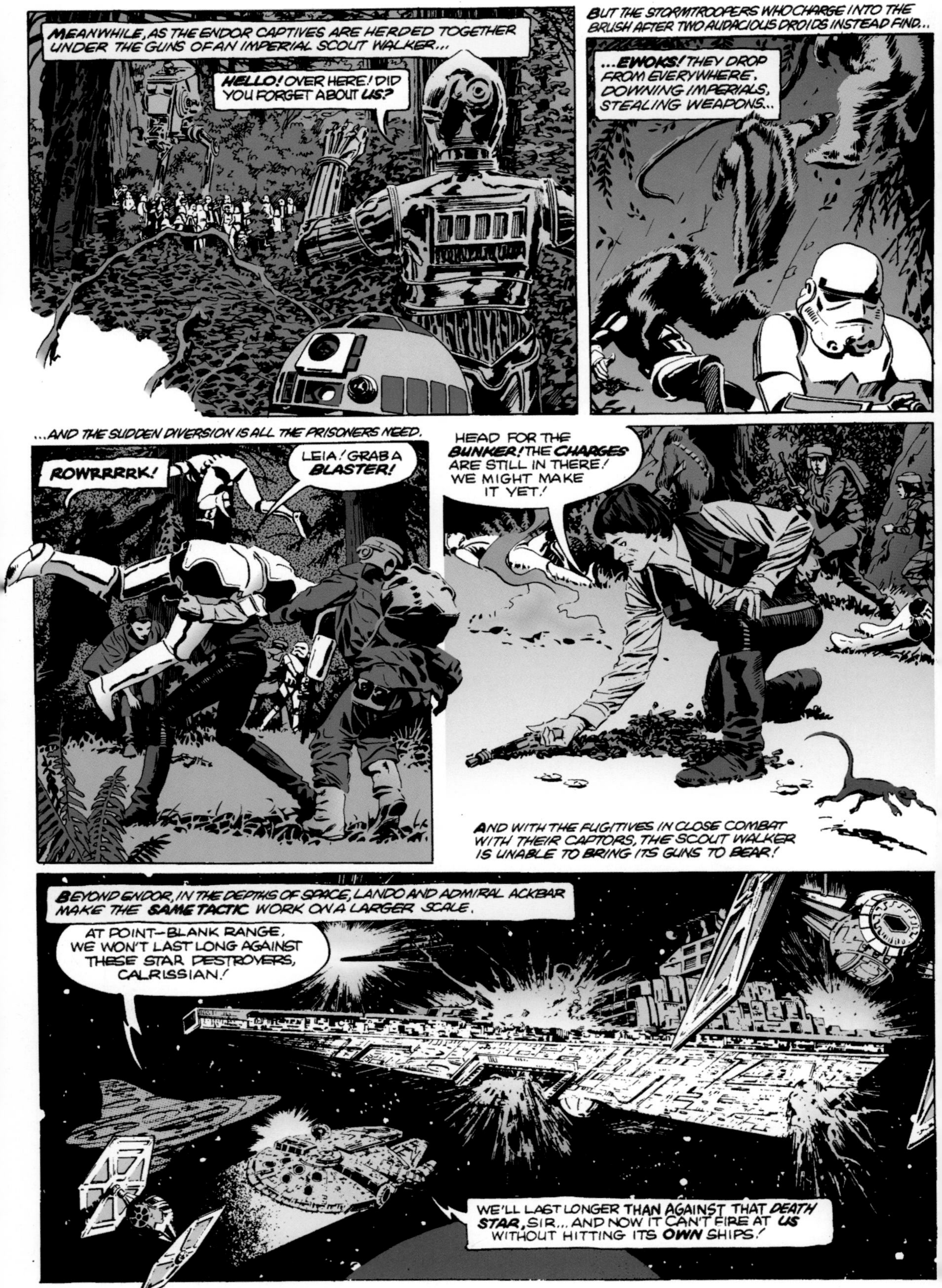
MEANWHILE, AS THE ENDOR CAPTIVES ARE HERDED TOGETHER UNDER THE GUNS OF AN IMPERIAL SCOUT WALKER...
HELLO! OVER HERE! DID YOU FORGET ABOUT US?
BUT THE STORMTROOPERS WHO CHARGE INTO THE BRUSH AFTER TWO AUDACIOUS DROIDS INSTEAD FIND...
...EWOKS! THEY DROP FROM EVERYWHERE, DOWNING IMPERIALS, STEALING WEAPONS...
...AND THE SUDDEN DIVERSION IS ALL THE PRISONERS NEED.
ROWRRRRK!
LEIA! GRAB A BLASTER!
HEAD FOR THE BUNKER! THE CHARGES ARE STILL IN THERE! WE MIGHT MAKE IT YET!
AND WITH THE FUGITIVES IN CLOSE COMBAT WITH THEIR CAPTORS, THE SCOUT WALKER IS UNABLE TO BRING ITS GUNS TO BEAR!
BEYOND ENDOR, IN THE DEPTHS OF SPACE, LANDO AND ADMIRAL ACKBAR MAKE THE SAME TACTIC WORK ON A LARGER SCALE.
AT POINT-BLANK RANGE, WE WON'T LAST LONG AGAINST THESE STAR DESTROYERS, CALRISSIAN!
WE'LL LAST LONGER THAN AGAINST THAT DEATH STAR, SIR... AND NOW IT CAN'T FIRE AT US WITHOUT HITTING ITS OWN SHIPS!

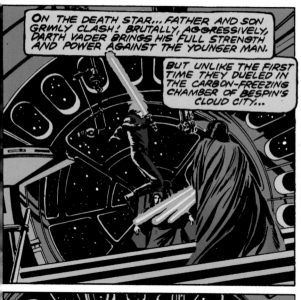

ON THE DEATH STAR... FATHER AND SON GRIMLY CLASH! BRUTALLY, AGGRESSIVELY, DARTH VADER BRINGS HIS FULL STRENGTH AND POWER AGAINST THE YOUNGER MAN.

BUT UNLIKE THE FIRST TIME THEY DUELED IN THE CARBON-FREEZING CHAMBER OF BESPIN'S CLOUD CITY...

...THIS IS A BATTLE OF EQUALS.

THE YOUNG JEDI HAS GROWN IN THE INTERIM...

...AND IF THERE IS ANY TRUE ADVANTAGE, IT SEEMS TO HAVE SHIFTED TO HIM.

THAT'S IT! USE YOUR AGGRESSIVE FEELINGS BOY! ATTACK! ATTACK! LET THE HATE FLOW THROUGH YOU!

BUT THE EMPEROR'S WORDS AWAKEN LUKE TO SOMETHING TERRIBLE RISING WITHIN HIM. HE STOPS... AND LOWERS HIS LIGHT-SABER.

I...I WILL NOT FIGHT YOU, FATHER. HERE...TAKE MY WEAPON.

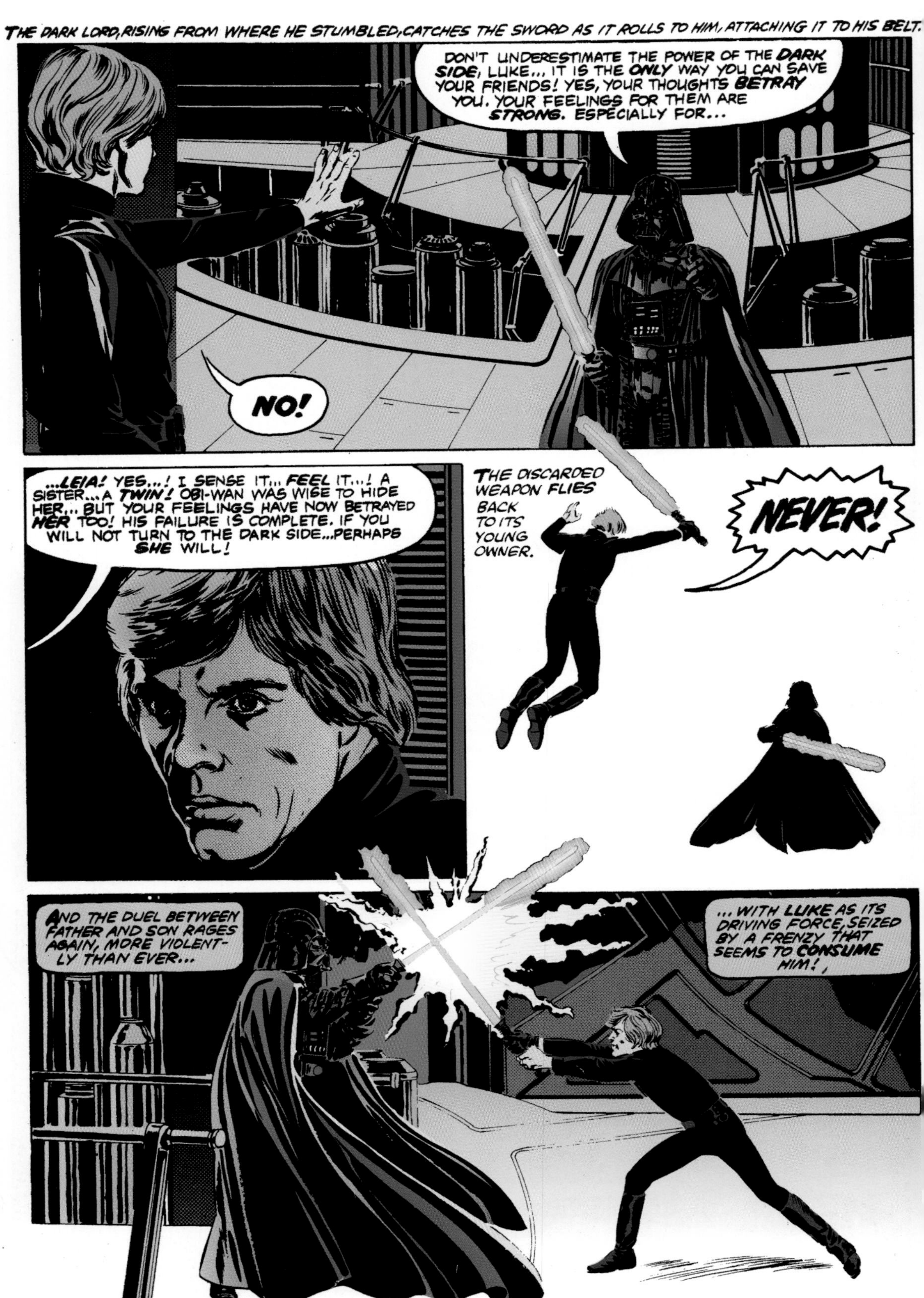
THE DARK LORD, RISING FROM WHERE HE STUMBLED, CATCHES THE SWORD AS IT ROLLS TO HIM, ATTACHING IT TO HIS BELT.
DON'T UNDERESTIMATE THE POWER OF THE DARK SIDE, LUKE... IT IS THE ONLY WAY YOU CAN SAVE YOUR FRIENDS! YES, YOUR THOUGHTS BETRAY YOU. YOUR FEELINGS FOR THEM ARE STRONG. ESPECIALLY FOR...
NO!
...LEIA! YES...! I SENSE IT... FEEL IT...! A SISTER... A TWIN! OBI-WAN WAS WISE TO HIDE HER... BUT YOUR FEELINGS HAVE NOW BETRAYED HER TOO! HIS FAILURE IS COMPLETE. IF YOU WILL NOT TURN TO THE DARK SIDE...PERHAPS SHE WILL!
THE DISCARDED WEAPON FLIES BACK TO ITS YOUNG OWNER.
NEVER!
AND THE DUEL BETWEEN FATHER AND SON RAGES AGAIN, MORE VIOLENTLY THAN EVER...
...WITH LUKE AS ITS DRIVING FORCE, SEIZED BY A FRENZY THAT SEEMS TO CONSUME HIM!

MEANWHILE, **WAR** HAS COME TO THE SANCTUARY MOON OF ENDOR, AND THOUGH THE WAGING OF WAR IS WHAT THE EMPIRE DOES BEST, **THIS** FIGHTING IS NOT WHAT IMPERIAL TROOPS ARE PREPARED FOR...

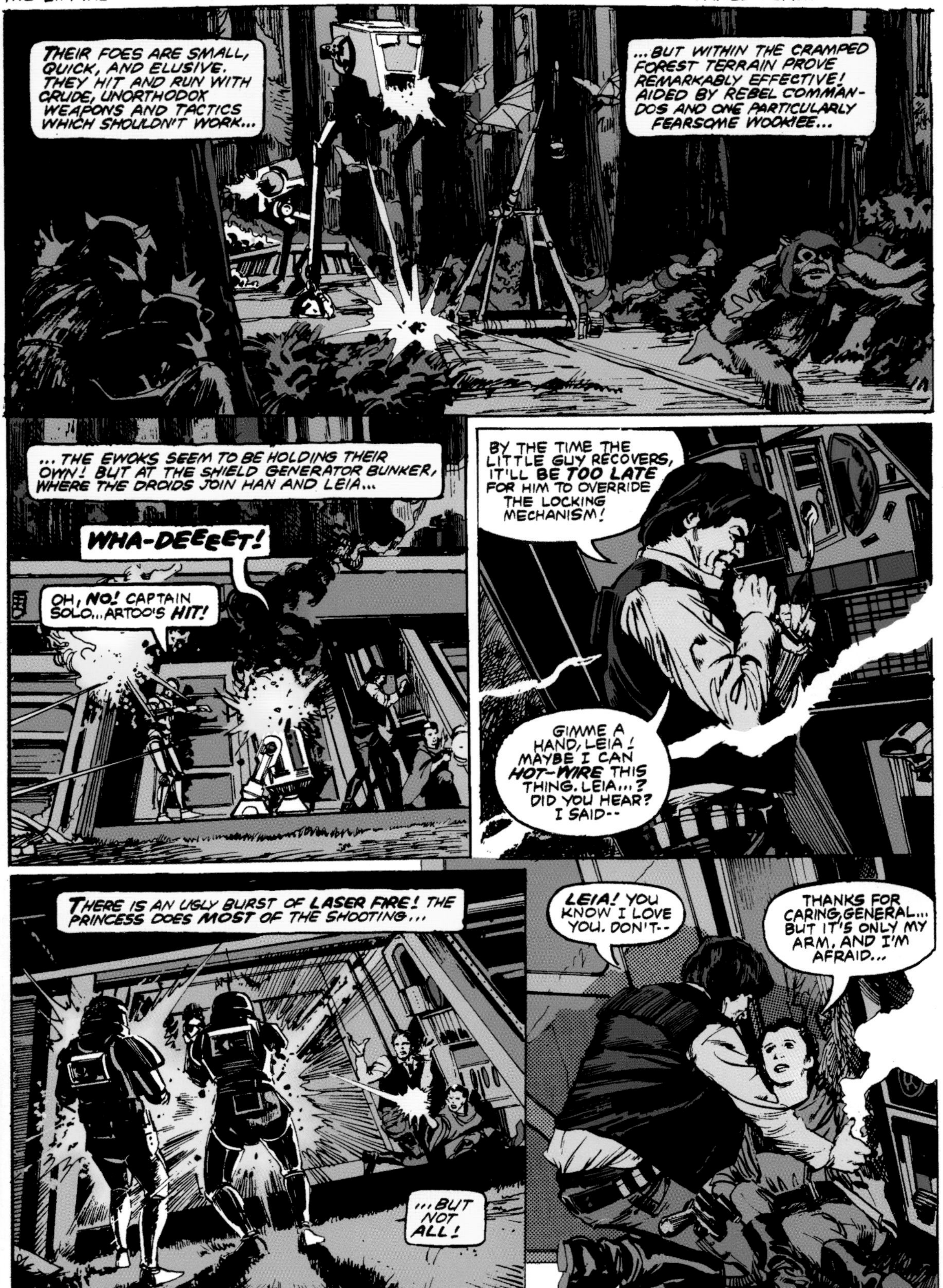
THEIR FOES ARE SMALL, QUICK, AND ELUSIVE. THEY HIT AND RUN WITH CRUDE, UNORTHODOX WEAPONS AND TACTICS WHICH SHOULDN'T WORK...
...BUT WITHIN THE CRAMPED FOREST TERRAIN PROVE REMARKABLY EFFECTIVE! AIDED BY REBEL COMMANDOS AND ONE PARTICULARLY FEARSOME WOOKIEE...
...THE EWOKS SEEM TO BE HOLDING THEIR OWN! BUT AT THE SHIELD GENERATOR BUNKER, WHERE THE DROIDS JOIN HAN AND LEIA...
WHA-DEEEEET!
OH, NO! CAPTAIN SOLO... ARTOO'S HIT!
BY THE TIME THE LITTLE GUY RECOVERS, IT'LL BE TOO LATE FOR HIM TO OVERRIDE THE LOCKING MECHANISM!
GIMME A HAND, LEIA! MAYBE I CAN HOT-WIRE THIS THING. LEIA...? DID YOU HEAR? I SAID--
THERE IS AN UGLY BURST OF LASER FIRE! THE PRINCESS DOES MOST OF THE SHOOTING...
...BUT NOT ALL!
LEIA! YOU KNOW I LOVE YOU. DON'T--
THANKS FOR CARING, GENERAL... BUT IT'S ONLY MY ARM, AND I'M AFRAID...

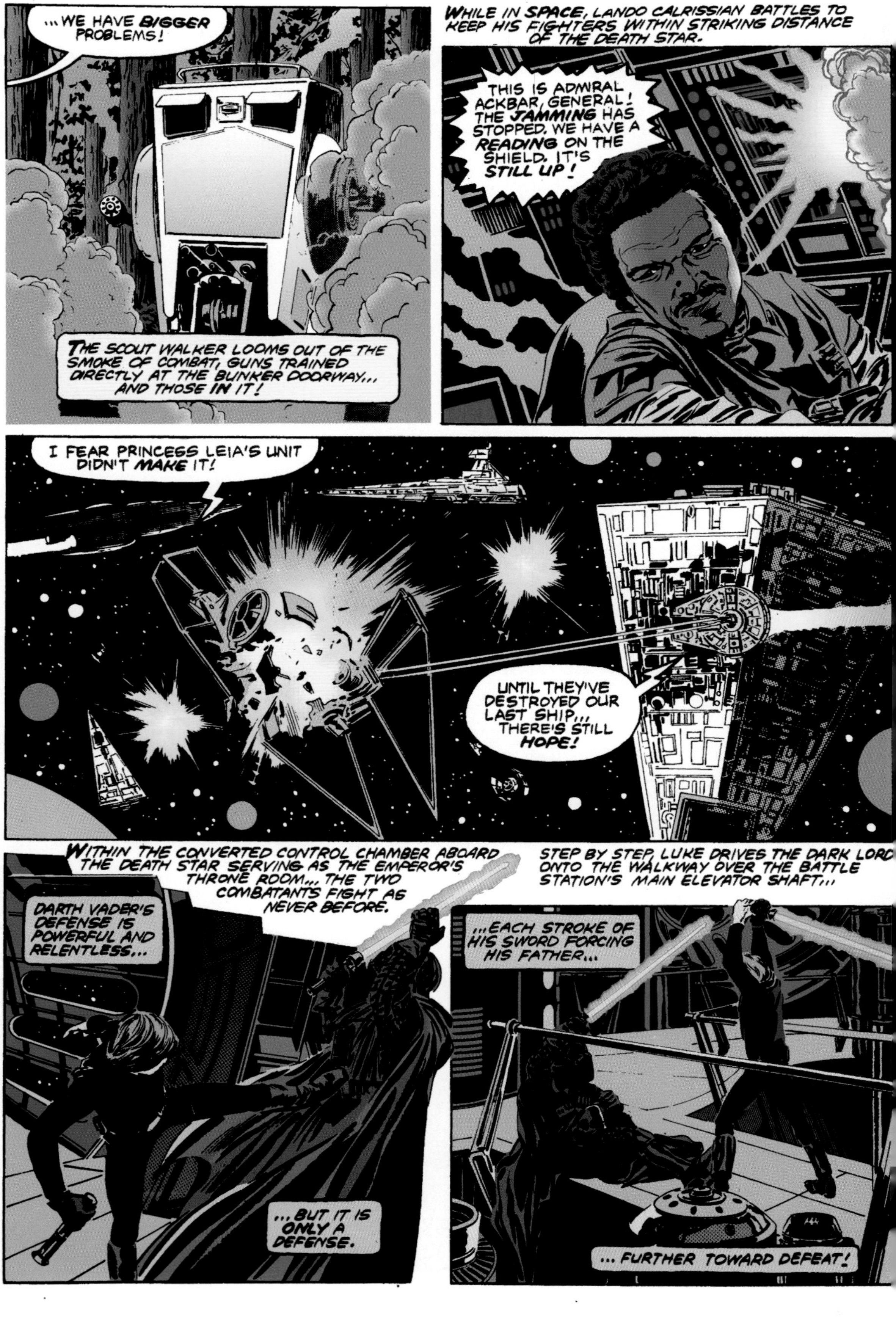

...WE HAVE BIGGER PROBLEMS!
THE SCOUT WALKER LOOMS OUT OF THE SMOKE OF COMBAT, GUNS TRAINED DIRECTLY AT THE BUNKER DOORWAY... AND THOSE IN IT!
WHILE IN SPACE, LANDO CALRISSIAN BATTLES TO KEEP HIS FIGHTERS WITHIN STRIKING DISTANCE OF THE DEATH STAR.
THIS IS ADMIRAL ACKBAR, GENERAL! THE JAMMING HAS STOPPED. WE HAVE A READING ON THE SHIELD. IT'S STILL UP!
I FEAR PRINCESS LEIA'S UNIT DIDN'T MAKE IT!
UNTIL THEY'VE DESTROYED OUR LAST SHIP... THERE'S STILL HOPE!
WITHIN THE CONVERTED CONTROL CHAMBER ABOARD THE DEATH STAR SERVING AS THE EMPEROR'S THRONE ROOM... THE TWO COMBATANTS FIGHT AS NEVER BEFORE.
DARTH VADER'S DEFENSE IS POWERFUL AND RELENTLESS...
...BUT IT IS ONLY A DEFENSE.
STEP BY STEP, LUKE DRIVES THE DARK LORD ONTO THE WALKWAY OVER THE BATTLE STATION'S MAIN ELEVATOR SHAFT...
...EACH STROKE OF HIS SWORD FORCING HIS FATHER...
... FURTHER TOWARD DEFEAT!

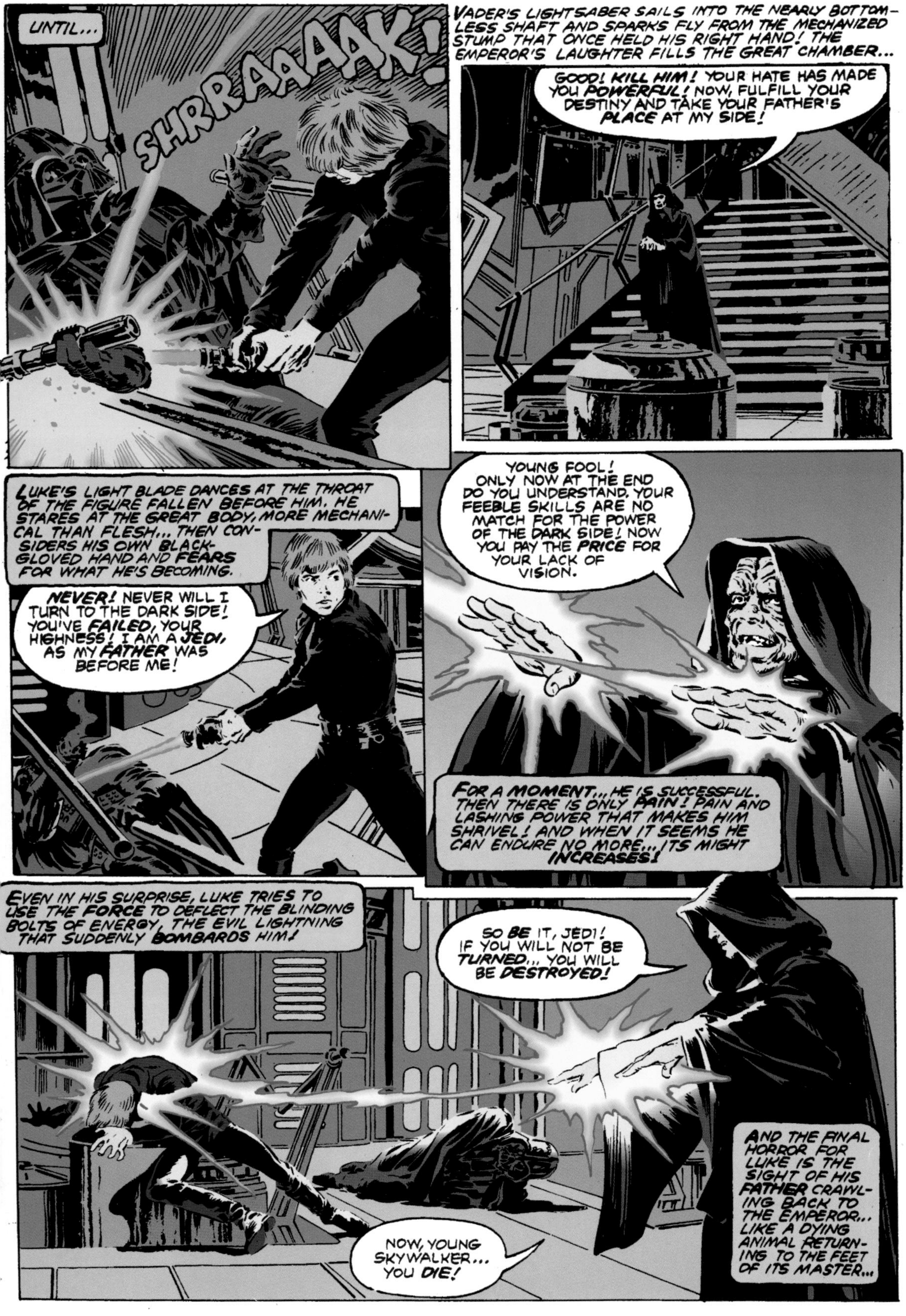
UNTIL...
SHRRAAAAK!
VADER'S LIGHTSABER SAILS INTO THE NEARLY BOTTOMLESS SHAFT AND SPARKS FLY FROM THE MECHANIZED STUMP THAT ONCE HELD HIS RIGHT HAND! THE EMPEROR'S LAUGHTER FILLS THE GREAT CHAMBER...
GOOD! KILL HIM! YOUR HATE HAS MADE YOU POWERFUL! NOW, FULFILL YOUR DESTINY AND TAKE YOUR FATHER'S PLACE AT MY SIDE!
LUKE'S LIGHT BLADE DANCES AT THE THROAT OF THE FIGURE FALLEN BEFORE HIM. HE STARES AT THE GREAT BODY, MORE MECHANICAL THAN FLESH... THEN CONSIDERS HIS OWN BLACK-GLOVED HAND AND FEARS FOR WHAT HE'S BECOMING.
NEVER! NEVER WILL I TURN TO THE DARK SIDE! YOU'VE FAILED, YOUR HIGHNESS! I AM A JEDI, AS MY FATHER WAS BEFORE ME!
YOUNG FOOL! ONLY NOW AT THE END DO YOU UNDERSTAND. YOUR FEEBLE SKILLS ARE NO MATCH FOR THE POWER OF THE DARK SIDE! NOW YOU PAY THE PRICE FOR YOUR LACK OF VISION.
FOR A MOMENT... HE IS SUCCESSFUL. THEN THERE IS ONLY PAIN! PAIN AND LASHING POWER THAT MAKES HIM SHRIVEL! AND WHEN IT SEEMS HE CAN ENDURE NO MORE... ITS MIGHT INCREASES!
EVEN IN HIS SURPRISE, LUKE TRIES TO USE THE FORCE TO DEFLECT THE BLINDING BOLTS OF ENERGY, THE EVIL LIGHTNING THAT SUDDENLY BOMBARDS HIM!
SO BE IT, JEDI! IF YOU WILL NOT BE TURNED... YOU WILL BE DESTROYED!
NOW, YOUNG SKYWALKER... YOU DIE!
AND THE FINAL HORROR FOR LUKE IS THE SIGHT OF HIS FATHER CRAWLING BACK TO THE EMPEROR... LIKE A DYING ANIMAL RETURNING TO THE FEET OF ITS MASTER...

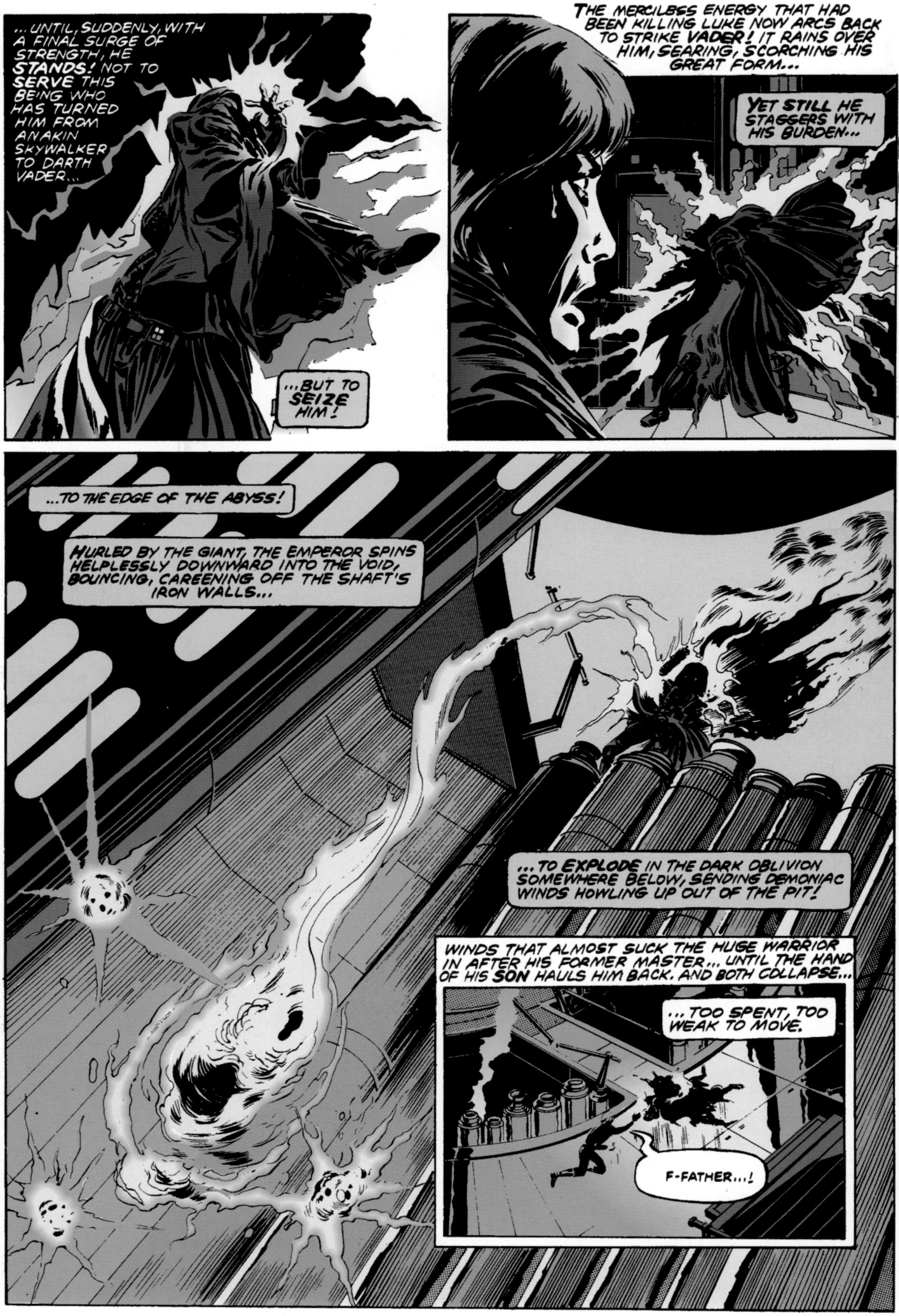
...UNTIL, SUDDENLY, WITH A FINAL SURGE OF STRENGTH, HE STANDS! NOT TO SERVE THIS BEING WHO HAS TURNED HIM FROM ANAKIN SKYWALKER TO DARTH VADER...
...BUT TO SEIZE HIM!
THE MERCILESS ENERGY THAT HAD BEEN KILLING LUKE NOW ARCS BACK TO STRIKE VADER! IT RAINS OVER HIM, SEARING, SCORCHING HIS GREAT FORM...
YET STILL HE STAGGERS WITH HIS BURDEN...
...TO THE EDGE OF THE ABYSS!
HURLED BY THE GIANT, THE EMPEROR SPINS HELPLESSLY DOWNWARD INTO THE VOID, BOUNCING, CAREENING OFF THE SHAFT'S IRON WALLS...
...TO EXPLODE IN THE DARK OBLIVION SOMEWHERE BELOW, SENDING DEMONIAC WINDS HOWLING UP OUT OF THE PIT!
WINDS THAT ALMOST SUCK THE HUGE WARRIOR IN AFTER HIS FORMER MASTER... UNTIL THE HAND OF HIS SON HAULS HIM BACK. AND BOTH COLLAPSE...
...TOO SPENT, TOO WEAK TO MOVE.
F-FATHER...!

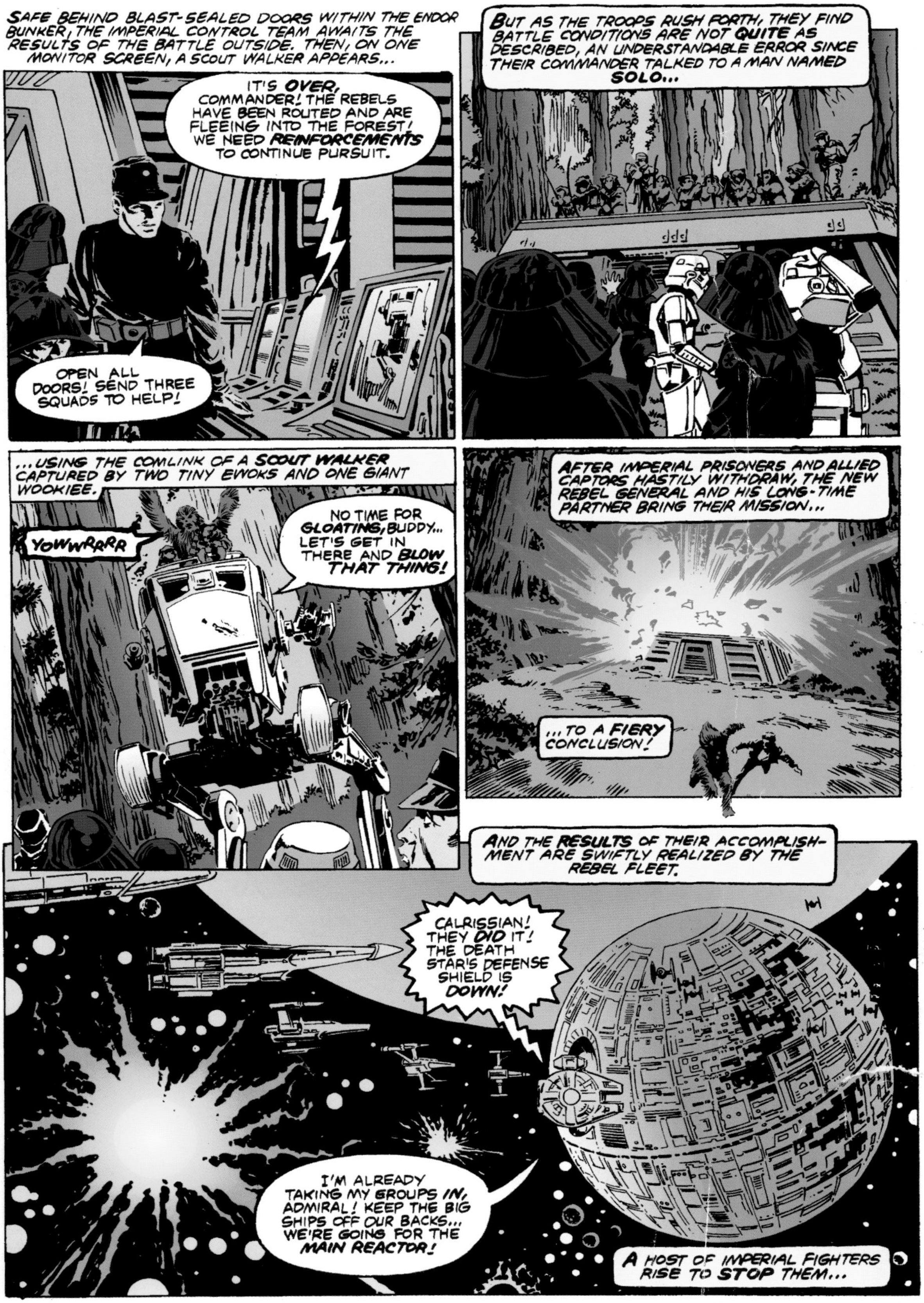
SAFE BEHIND BLAST-SEALED DOORS WITHIN THE ENDOR BUNKER, THE IMPERIAL CONTROL TEAM AWAITS THE RESULTS OF THE BATTLE OUTSIDE. THEN, ON ONE MONITOR SCREEN, A SCOUT WALKER APPEARS...
IT'S OVER, COMMANDER! THE REBELS HAVE BEEN ROUTED AND ARE FLEEING INTO THE FOREST! WE NEED REINFORCEMENTS TO CONTINUE PURSUIT.
OPEN ALL DOORS! SEND THREE SQUADS TO HELP!
BUT AS THE TROOPS RUSH FORTH, THEY FIND BATTLE CONDITIONS ARE NOT QUITE AS DESCRIBED, AN UNDERSTANDABLE ERROR SINCE THEIR COMMANDER TALKED TO A MAN NAMED SOLO...
...USING THE COMLINK OF A SCOUT WALKER CAPTURED BY TWO TINY EWOKS AND ONE GIANT WOOKIEE.
YOWWRRRR
NO TIME FOR GLOATING, BUDDY... LET'S GET IN THERE AND BLOW THAT THING!
AFTER IMPERIAL PRISONERS AND ALLIED CAPTORS HASTILY WITHDRAW, THE NEW REBEL GENERAL AND HIS LONG-TIME PARTNER BRING THEIR MISSION...
...TO A FIERY CONCLUSION!
AND THE RESULTS OF THEIR ACCOMPLISHMENT ARE SWIFTLY REALIZED BY THE REBEL FLEET.
CALRISSIAN! THEY DID IT! THE DEATH STAR'S DEFENSE SHIELD IS DOWN!
I'M ALREADY TAKING MY GROUPS IN, ADMIRAL! KEEP THE BIG SHIPS OFF OUR BACKS... WE'RE GOING FOR THE MAIN REACTOR!
A HOST OF IMPERIAL FIGHTERS RISE TO STOP THEM...

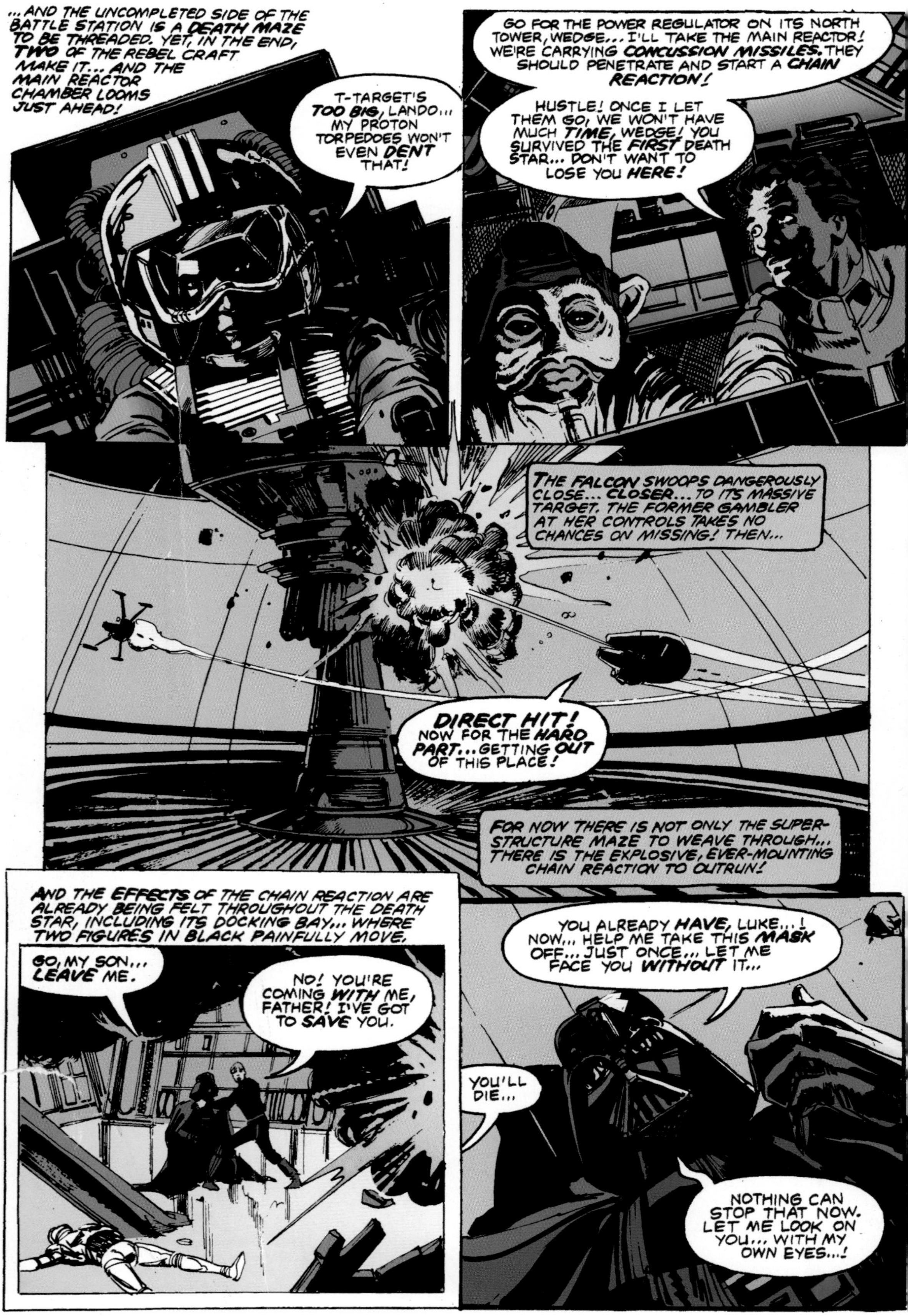
...AND THE UNCOMPLETED SIDE OF THE BATTLE STATION IS A DEATH MAZE TO BE THREADED. YET, IN THE END, TWO OF THE REBEL CRAFT MAKE IT... AND THE MAIN REACTOR CHAMBER LOOMS JUST AHEAD!
T-TARGET'S TOO BIG, LANDO... MY PROTON TORPEDOES WON'T EVEN DENT THAT!
GO FOR THE POWER REGULATOR ON ITS NORTH TOWER, WEDGE... I'LL TAKE THE MAIN REACTOR! WE'RE CARRYING CONCUSSION MISSILES. THEY SHOULD PENETRATE AND START A CHAIN REACTION!
HUSTLE! ONCE I LET THEM GO, WE WON'T HAVE MUCH TIME, WEDGE! YOU SURVIVED THE FIRST DEATH STAR... DON'T WANT TO LOSE YOU HERE!
THE FALCON SWOOPS DANGEROUSLY CLOSE... CLOSER... TO ITS MASSIVE TARGET. THE FORMER GAMBLER AT HER CONTROLS TAKES NO CHANCES ON MISSING! THEN...
DIRECT HIT! NOW FOR THE HARD PART... GETTING OUT OF THIS PLACE!
FOR NOW THERE IS NOT ONLY THE SUPER-STRUCTURE MAZE TO WEAVE THROUGH... THERE IS THE EXPLOSIVE, EVER-MOUNTING CHAIN REACTION TO OUTRUN!
AND THE EFFECTS OF THE CHAIN REACTION ARE ALREADY BEING FELT THROUGHOUT THE DEATH STAR, INCLUDING ITS DOCKING BAY... WHERE TWO FIGURES IN BLACK PAINFULLY MOVE.
GO, MY SON... LEAVE ME.
NO! YOU'RE COMING WITH ME, FATHER! I'VE GOT TO SAVE YOU.
YOU'LL DIE...
YOU ALREADY HAVE, LUKE...! NOW... HELP ME TAKE THIS MASK OFF... JUST ONCE... LET ME FACE YOU WITHOUT IT...
NOTHING CAN STOP THAT NOW. LET ME LOOK ON YOU... WITH MY OWN EYES...!

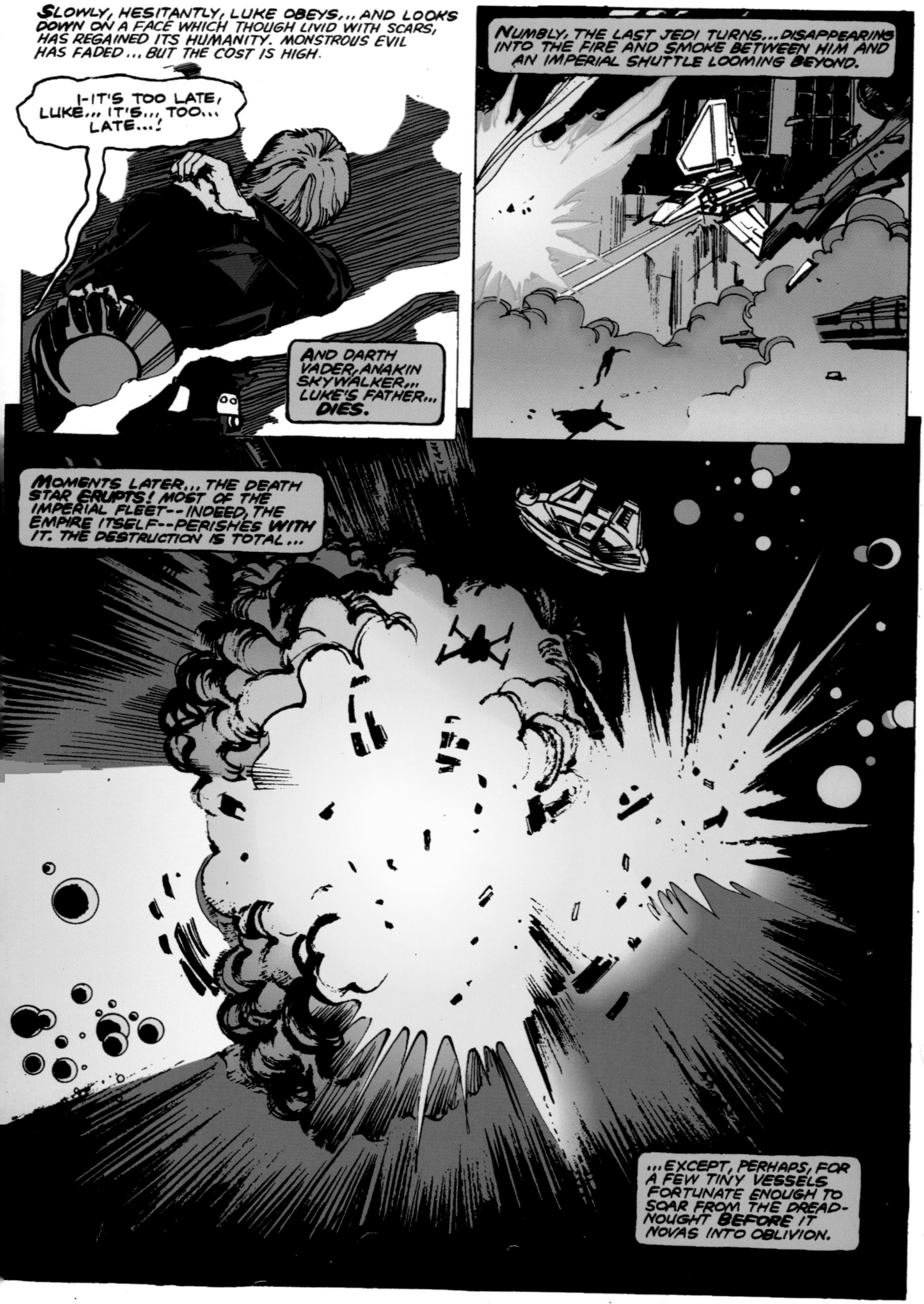
SLOWLY, HESITANTLY, LUKE OBEYS... AND LOOKS DOWN ON A FACE WHICH THOUGH LIVID WITH SCARS, HAS REGAINED ITS HUMANITY. MONSTROUS EVIL HAS FADED... BUT THE COST IS HIGH.
I-IT'S TOO LATE, LUKE... IT'S... TOO... LATE...!
AND DARTH VADER, ANAKIN SKYWALKER... LUKE'S FATHER... DIES.
NUMBLY, THE LAST JEDI TURNS... DISAPPEARING INTO THE FIRE AND SMOKE BETWEEN HIM AND AN IMPERIAL SHUTTLE LOOMING BEYOND.
MOMENTS LATER... THE DEATH STAR ERUPTS! MOST OF THE IMPERIAL FLEET--INDEED, THE EMPIRE ITSELF--PERISHES WITH IT. THE DESTRUCTION IS TOTAL...
...EXCEPT, PERHAPS, FOR A FEW TINY VESSELS FORTUNATE ENOUGH TO SOAR FROM THE DREAD-NOUGHT BEFORE IT NOVAS INTO OBLIVION.

NIGHT ON ENDOR! A HUGE BONFIRE BURNS IN THE EWOK VILLAGE, THE CENTERPIECE OF A WILD CELEBRATION, AS REBELS AND THEIR ALLIES REJOICE IN ITS WARMTH.

MUSIC AND LAUGHTER SWELL.

PAST ANTAGONISMS AND MISUNDERSTANDINGS ARE FORGOTTEN.

OLD FRIENDS ARE REUNITED, AS ONE BY ONE THE WARRIORS RETURN...

...EVEN THOSE MOST FEARED FOREVER LOST.

AND IF LATER, WHILE THE REVELRY AROUND THE CAMPFIRE SWELLS, ONE AMONG THEM STANDS APART, HAUNTED, PERHAPS, BY KNOWLEDGE FEW OTHERS CAN EVER SHARE...

...HE IS STILL NOT ALONE.

THERE IS SOMEONE WAITING TO TAKE HIS ARM, TO DRAW HIM TO HER AND THE OTHERS...

...BACK INTO THE CIRCLE OF WARMTH AND LOVE

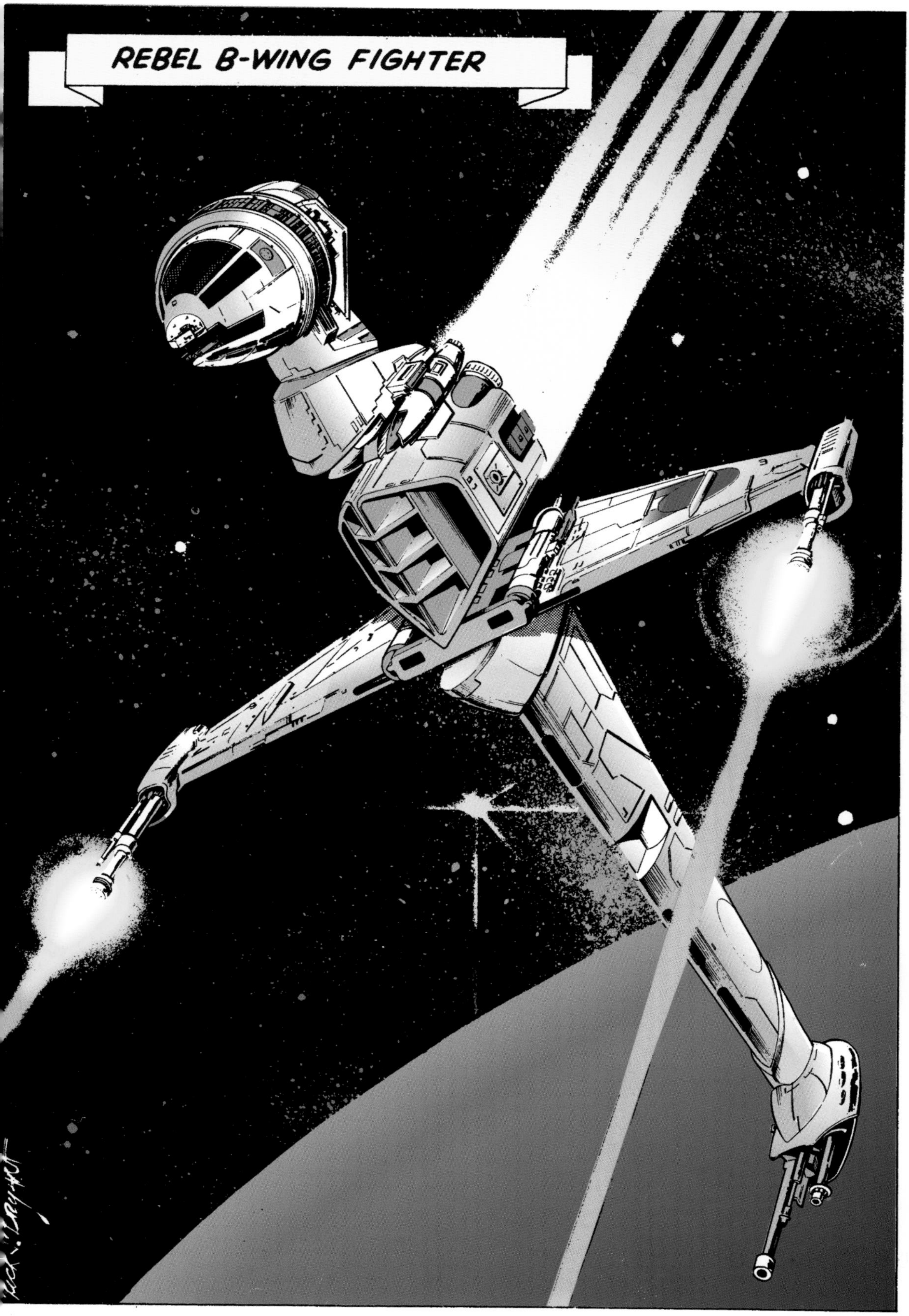
REBEL B-WING FIGHTER

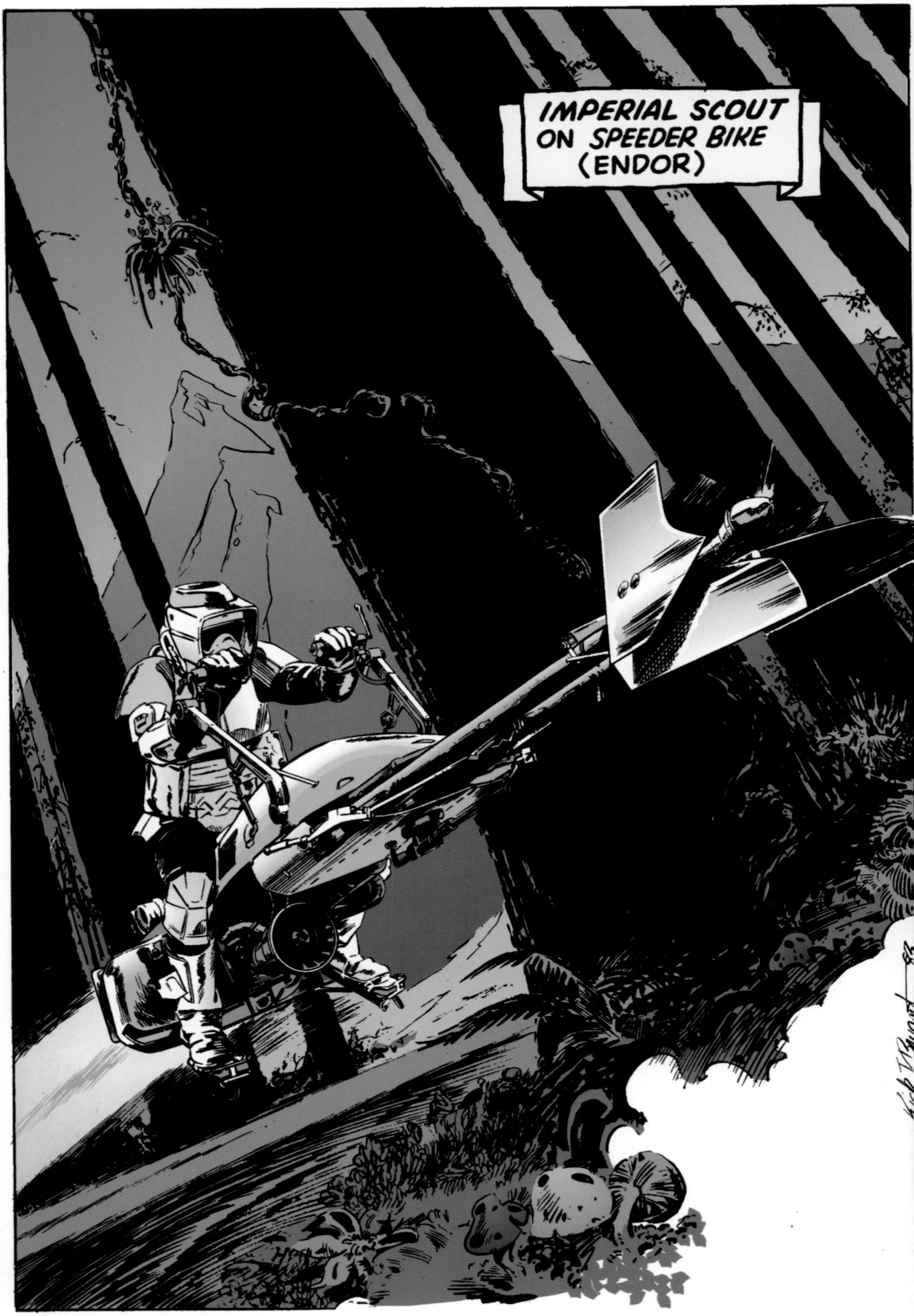
IMPERIAL SCOUT
ON SPEEDER BIKE
(ENDOR)

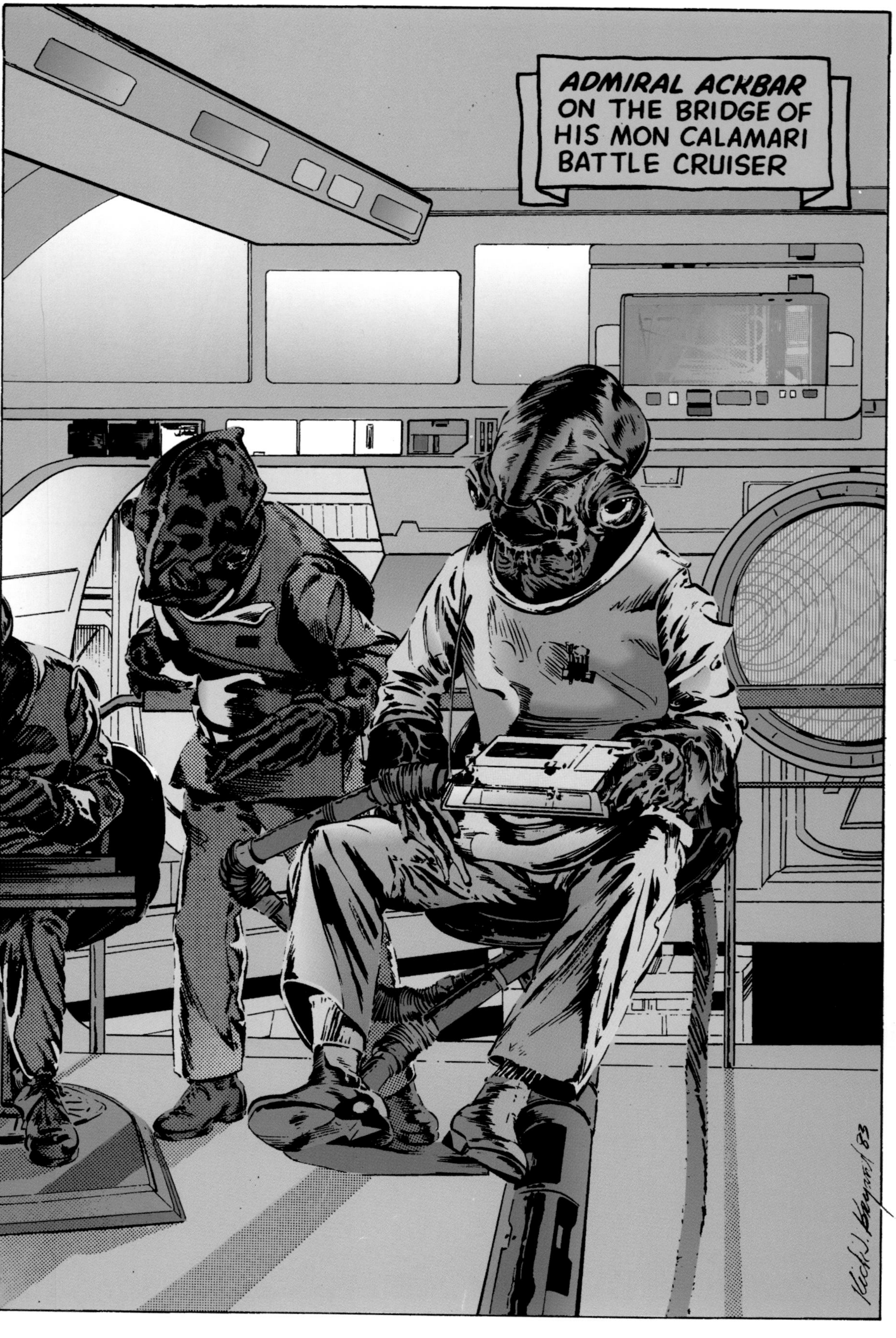
ADMIRAL ACKBAR
ON THE BRIDGE OF
HIS MON CALAMARI
BATTLE CRUISER

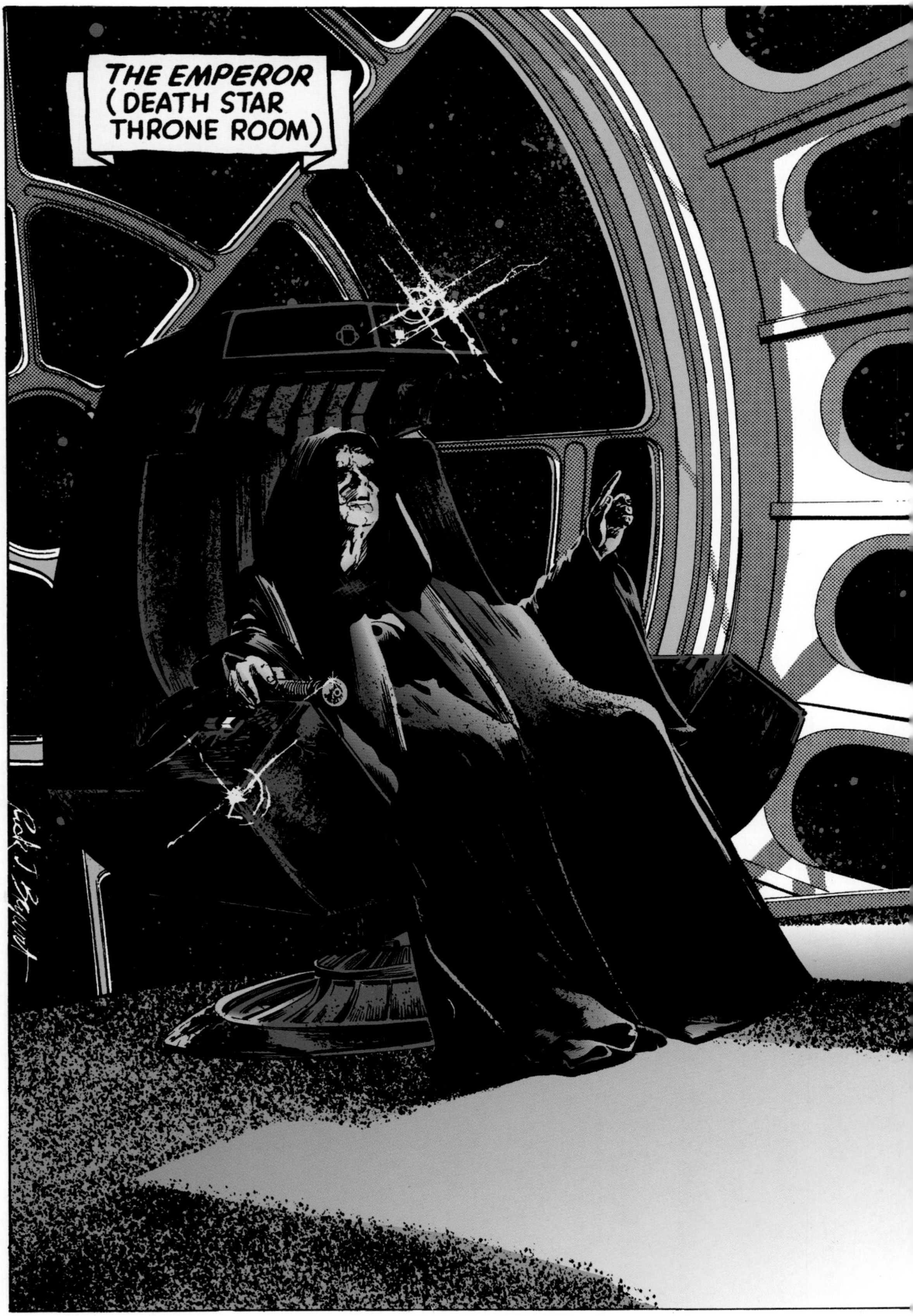
THE EMPEROR
(DEATH STAR
THRONE ROOM)